THANKS TO CEM AND
TO CRISP AUTUMN NIGHTS.

PORTIONS OF THIS BOOK PREVIOUSLY
APPEARED IN WARMER (ED. SAITO
AND WHITE) AND IN INKBRICK 10
(ED. ROTHMAN, TUNIS, SOKOLIN, HARVEY)

C000091642

BUT

THE FUTURE
IS SIGNIFICANT

IT HAS
TO BE

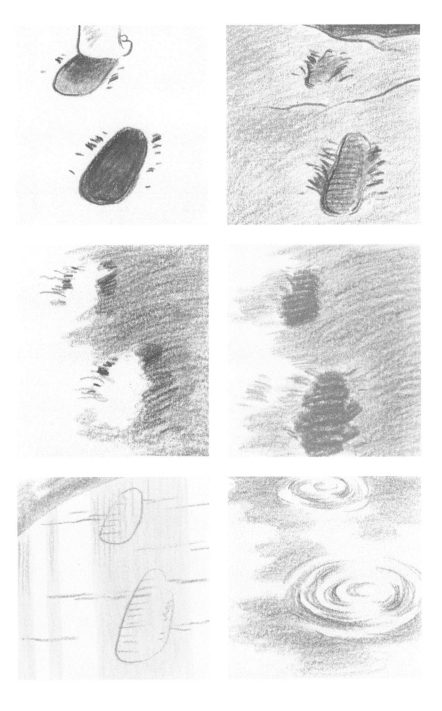

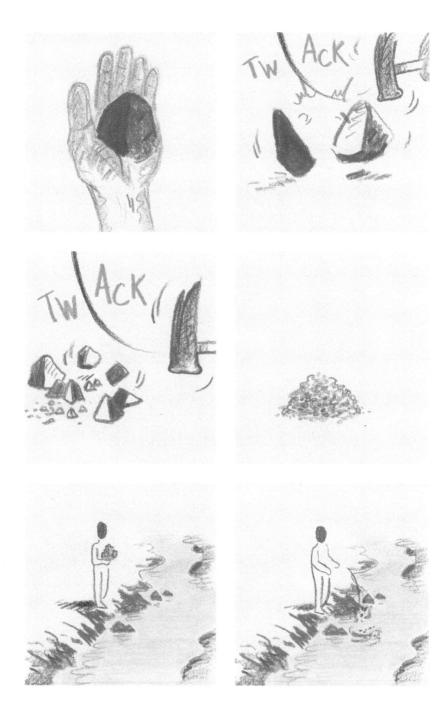

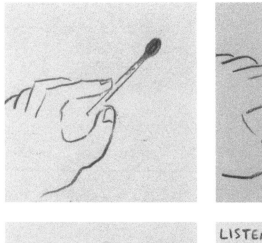

FOOM

LISTEN TO THE SOUND
OF THE EARTH TURNING

SHAKE

LISTEN TO THE SOUND
OF UNDERGROUND WATER

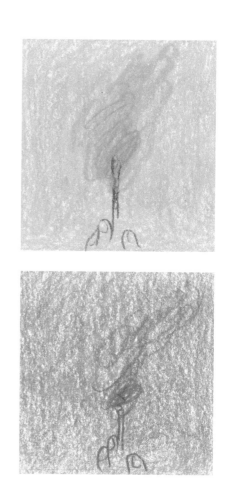

WATCH A HUNDRED YEAR
OLD TREE BREATHE

TURN

IMAGINE WATER COMING
DOWN A DRY RIVERBED

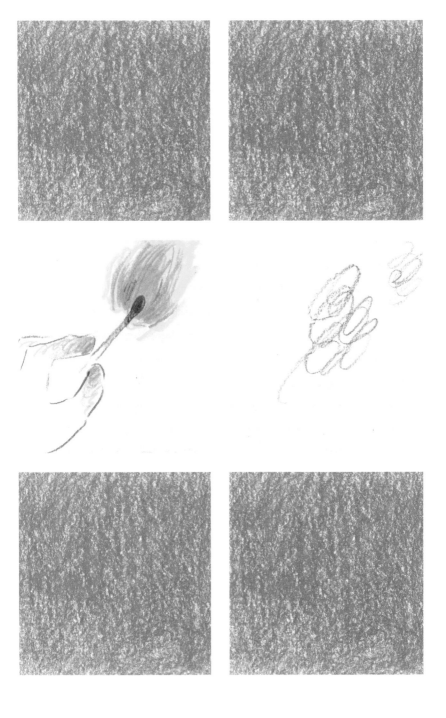

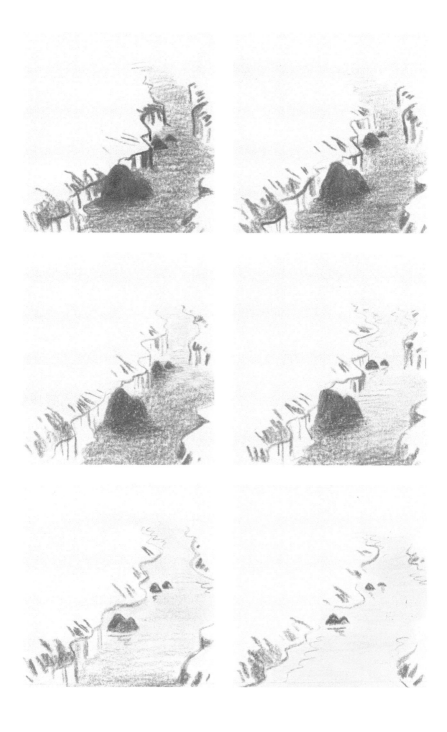

TRY NOT
TO MAKE
SOUNDS

HELLO

PICK UP A PENCIL
IF YOU WANT

AND FOLLOW ME

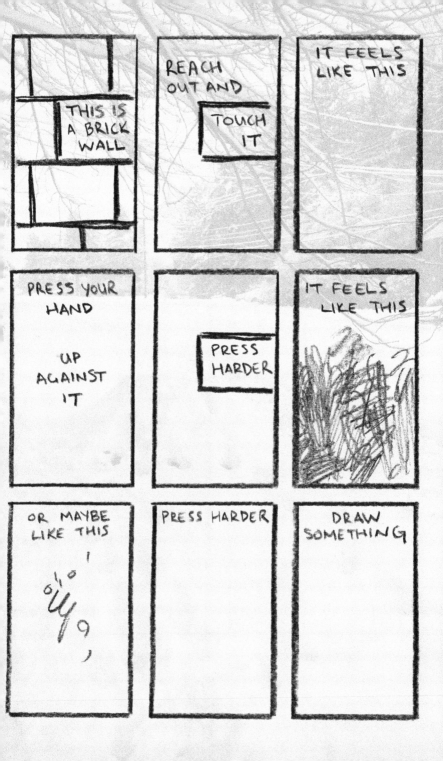

DRAW A CIRCLE.
DRAW IT AGAIN. MORE AGRESSIVELY.
NO, MORE LIKE:
NOW DRAW IT WITH CARE AND PRECISION. ALLOW YOUR HAND TO SLOWLY PURSUE THE GHOST OF YOUR OWN PAST MOVEMENTS.
AS WELL AS MINE.
DRAW IT AGAIN.

DRAW A SYMBOL.

DRAW IT AGAIN. NOW ASSOCIATE
WITH IT SOME MEANING.

DRAW IT AGAIN.

DRAW A LINE. LISTEN CAREFULLY TO
THE WAY IT SOUNDS.

DRAW THAT SOUND HERE.

IMAGINE
BLUE SKIES

BREATHE
DEEPLY.

IMAGINE
WHITE CLOUDS

IMAGINE AN IMAGE. CREATE IT, EMBODY
IT, REALIZE IT AS FULLY AS YOU
CAN IN YOUR MIND.

PAUSE. COLLECT YOURSELF.
RETAIN THE IMAGE.

CONSIDER CAREFULLY WHETHER OR
NOT YOU WOULD LIKE TO
DRAW THE IMAGE.

YOU HAVE SOMETHING ON YOUR MIND.
I CAN TELL. WRITE IT DOWN HERE.

NOW DRAW IT.

NOW DRAW IT
AGAIN. DIFFERENTLY.

NOW SAY IT OUT LOUD.

NOW TEAR THIS
PAGE OUT. DO IT
CAREFULLY.

WAIT! ARE YOU SURE?
HAVE YOU EVER MADE A
MISTAKE? HAVE YOU EVER
CAST OFF A MEMORY YOU
WISH YOU HAD INSTEAD
PRESERVED?

DRAW A LINE.

DRAW TWO LINES.

DRAW MORE LINES.
THEY DON'T HAVE
TO MEAN ANYTHING.
KEEP YOUR HAND
MOVING.

KEEP YOUR MIND
RACING.

KEEP YOUR BLOOD
FLOWING.

TAKE A DEEP
BREATH. PUSH
HARDER. DRAW
A SYMBOL.

IMAGINE
AN ICEBERG

IMAGINE IT FLOATING IN THE
WATER. IMAGINE HOW COLD IT
WOULD FEEL IF YOU TOUCHED
IT WITH YOUR BARE HANDS.

IT BROKE OFF THE LARSEN C
ICE SHELF IN JULY.

THE CRACK HAD BEEN GROWING
FOR YEARS, FASTER AND FASTER.
WE KNEW IT WAS COMING.

IMAGINE THE CRACK EXPANDING

NOW GO BACKWARDS - SEE IF
YOU CAN IMAGINE IT SHRINKING.

IMAGINE IT FLOATING
IN THE WATER.

THE WAVES LAPPING
UP AGAINST IT.

THE SUN SHIMMERING
ON ITS SURFACE.

IMAGINE THE WHITE ICE.

IMAGINE THE BLUE WATER.

NOW

IMAGINE IT RISING UP
OUT OF THE WATER.

IMAGINE IT MOVING
THROUGH THE AIR

AND COMING TO REST
DIRECTLY ABOVE YOU.

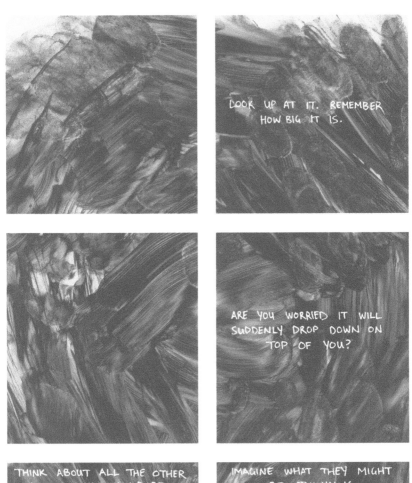

LOOK UP AT IT. REMEMBER
HOW BIG IT IS.

ARE YOU WORRIED IT WILL
SUDDENLY DROP DOWN ON
TOP OF YOU?

THINK ABOUT ALL THE OTHER
PEOPLE WHO WOULD BE
LOOKING UP AT IT TOO.

IMAGINE WHAT THEY MIGHT
BE THINKING.

TRY TO HOLD THESE THOUGHTS
IN YOUR MIND AS LONG
AS YOU CAN.

THINK ABOUT THE WATER.

THINK ABOUT THE ICE.

THE TWO GLACIERS MEET
SOMEWHERE IN THE MIDDLE
OF THE OCEAN.

OF COURSE, THEY'RE NOT
GLACIERS ANY MORE.
BUT THEY WERE ONCE.
AND THEY REMEMBER.

SO THEY INTERMINGLE, AND
THEY TALK ABOUT WHAT IT WAS
LIKE TO BE A GLACIER FOR
SO LONG AND THEN NOT BE
A GLACIER ANY MORE.

THEY TALK ABOUT THE
SUN AND THEY TALK
ABOUT MELTING.

THE TWO GLACIERS GLIDE
THROUGH THE WATER TOGETHER.
THEY CRASH INTO YOUR
BEACHES AND RAIN DOWN ON
YOUR HOMES AND SOMETIMES
FLOOD YOUR STREETS.

AS THEY DO THESE THINGS,
THEY'RE TALKING TO EACH
OTHER AND THEY'RE TRYING
TO TALK TO YOU. THEY SAY

"WE REMEMBER THAT WE WERE
GLACIERS ONCE, AND WE KNOW
THAT ONE DAY WE MIGHT
BE GLACIERS AGAIN."

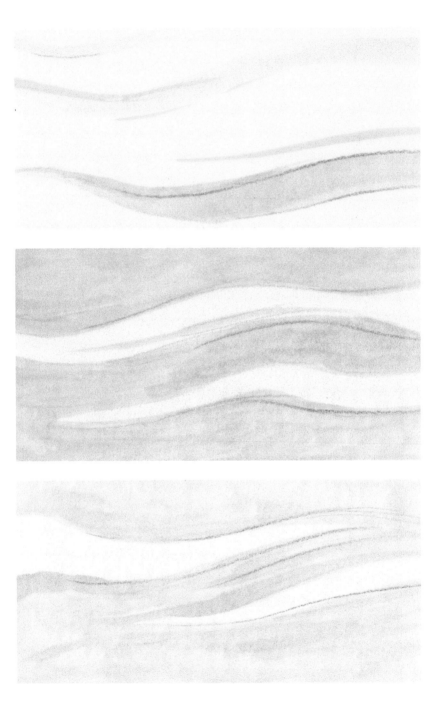

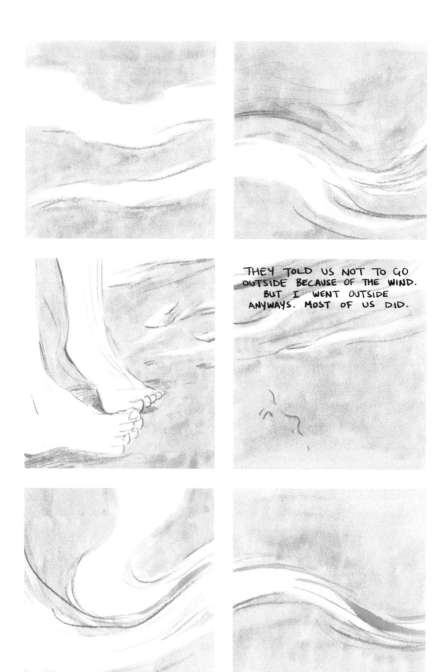

THEY TOLD US NOT TO GO OUTSIDE BECAUSE OF THE WIND. BUT I WENT OUTSIDE ANYWAYS. MOST OF US DID.

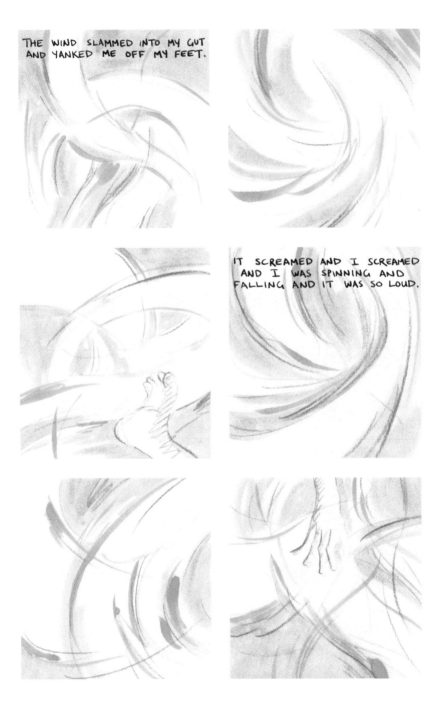

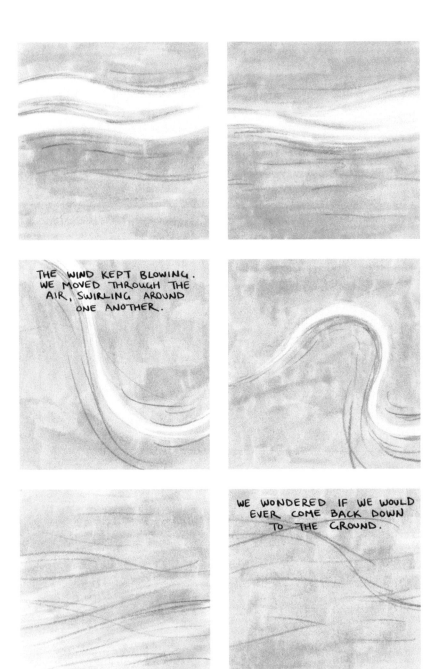

THE WIND KEPT BLOWING.
WE MOVED THROUGH THE
AIR, SWIRLING AROUND
ONE ANOTHER.

WE WONDERED IF WE WOULD
EVER COME BACK DOWN
TO THE GROUND.

DRAW THE SOUND
OF THE ROOM

DRAW THE SMELL
OF THE ROOM

DRAW THE FEELING
OF SOMEONE YOU
LOVE COMING INTO
THE ROOM WHEN YOU
FEEL SMALL
AND BROKEN

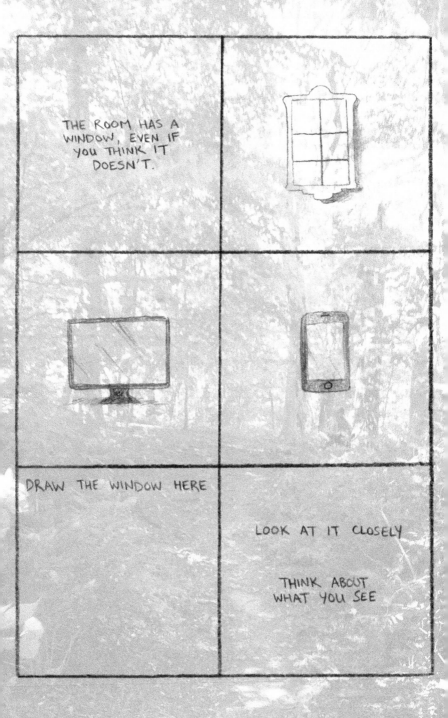

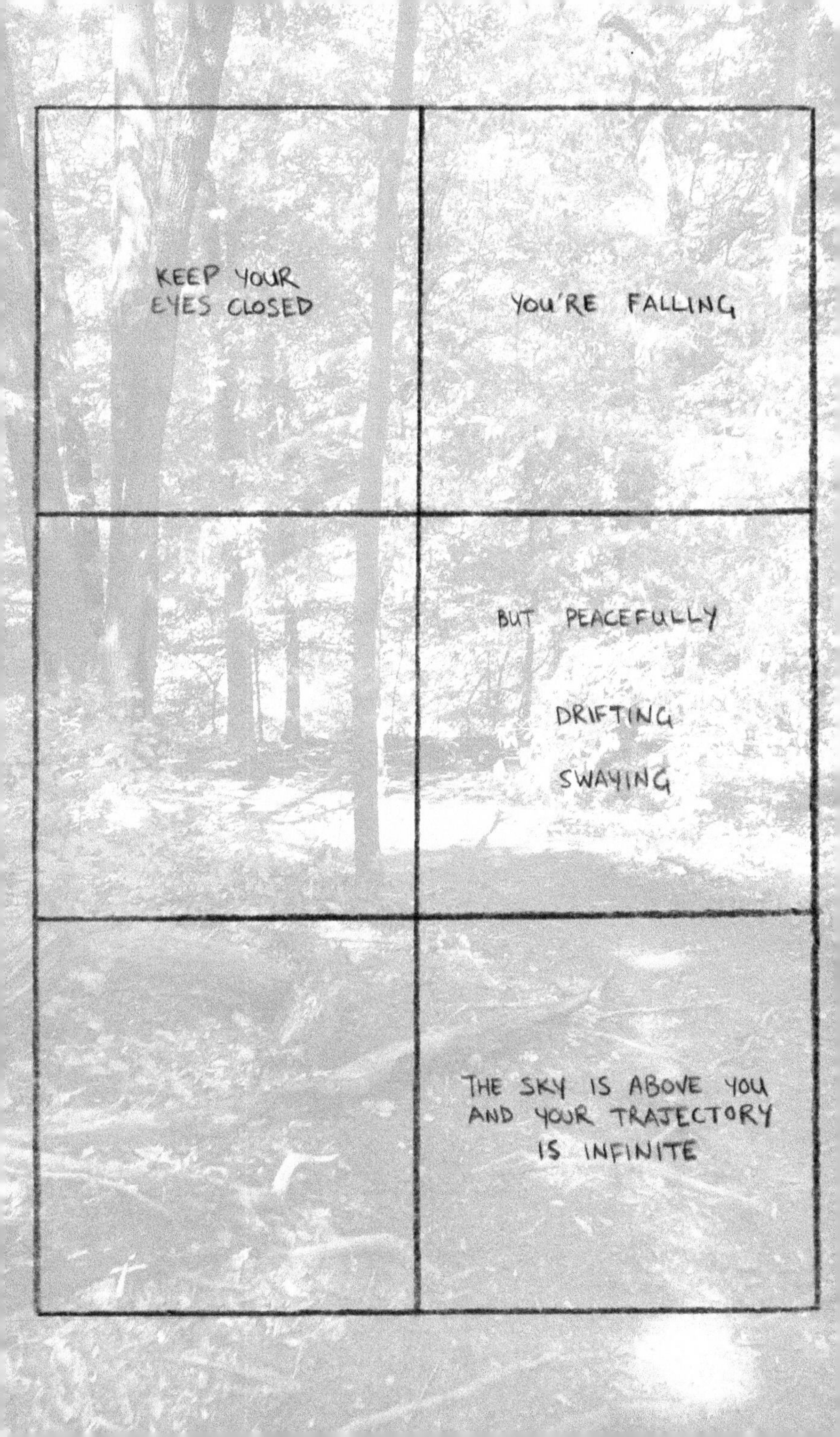

KEEP YOUR
EYES CLOSED

YOU'RE FALLING

BUT PEACEFULLY

DRIFTING

SWAYING

THE SKY IS ABOVE YOU
AND YOUR TRAJECTORY
IS INFINITE

SIT IN THE ROOM FOR
AS LONG AS YOU CAN

PEOPLE WILL TELL YOU
THAT IMPORTANT THINGS
ARE HAPPENING
OUTSIDE THE ROOM.

BUT IMPORTANT THINGS
ARE HAPPENING INSIDE THE
ROOM TOO.

SO KEEP WAITING

YOU SAY YOU DON'T
HAVE TIME, BUT YOU
HAVE TIME NOW.

DON'T WORRY

I'LL TELL YOU IF
ANYONE IS
LOOKING FOR YOU.

FIND THE CENTER
OF THE ROOM

DRAW A CIRCLE
AROUND YOURSELF

AND DO NOT
LEAVE THE CIRCLE

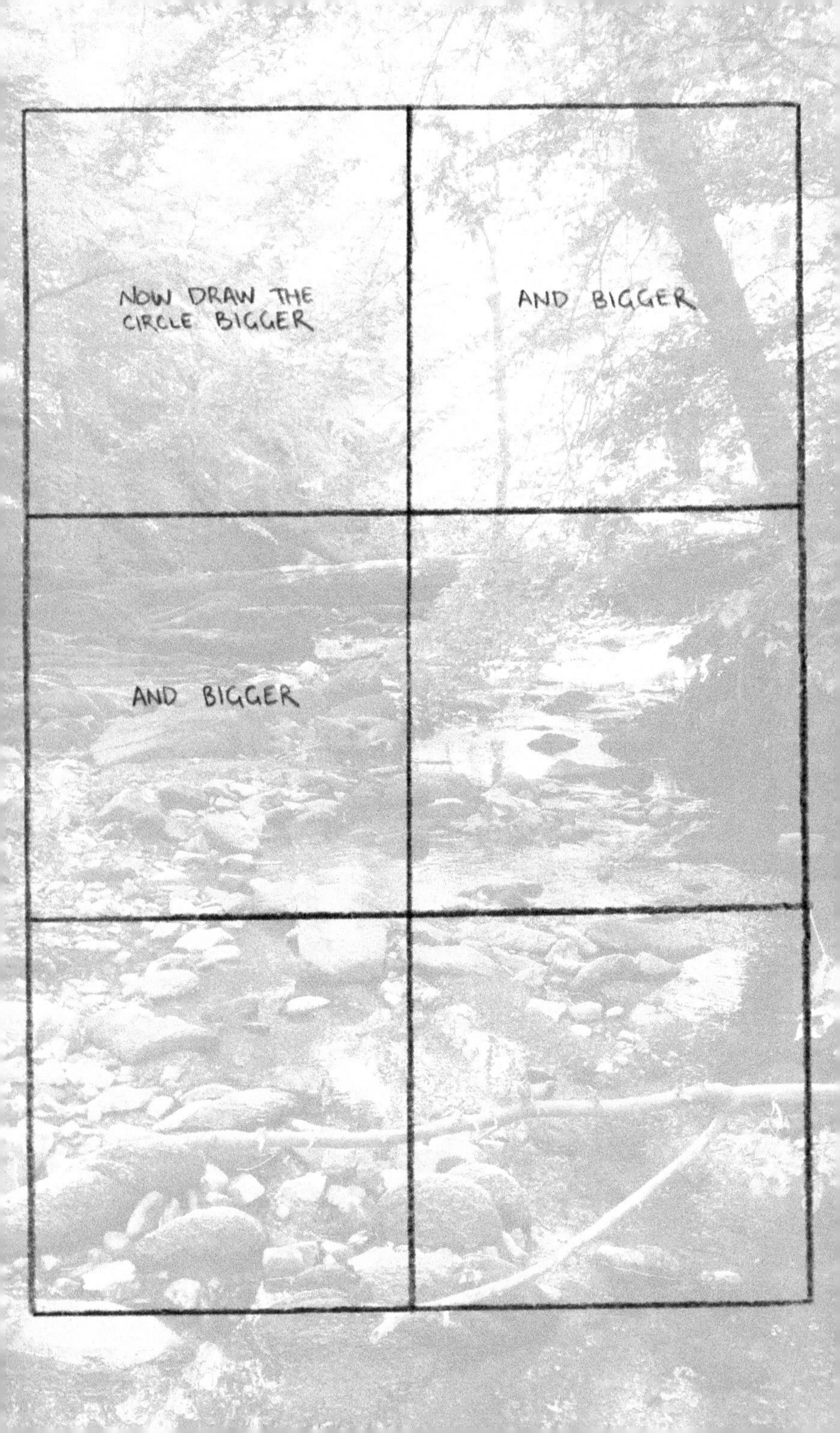
NOW DRAW THE CIRCLE BIGGER
AND BIGGER
AND BIGGER

NOW

REACH YOUR HAND OUT

AND COME WITH ME

SELECT THE SHAPE OF YOUR WORRIES
OTHER (DRAW HERE)
NOW, PUT THOSE WORRIES ASIDE. DON'T THINK ABOUT THEM FOR NOW.

SELECT THE DIRECTION
OF YOUR FEAR

OTHER (DRAW HERE)

BUT RIGHT NOW YOU'RE
JUST SITTING HERE. YOU
HAVE NOTHING TO FEAR.

DRAW THE SIZE OF THE UNKNOWN. YOU MAY
NEED MORE PAPER.

YOU WANT TO STAND
UP. DON'T STAND UP.

YOU'LL HAVE TO START
WALKING EVENTUALLY.

BUT FOR NOW, YOU CAN
SIT HERE WITH ME

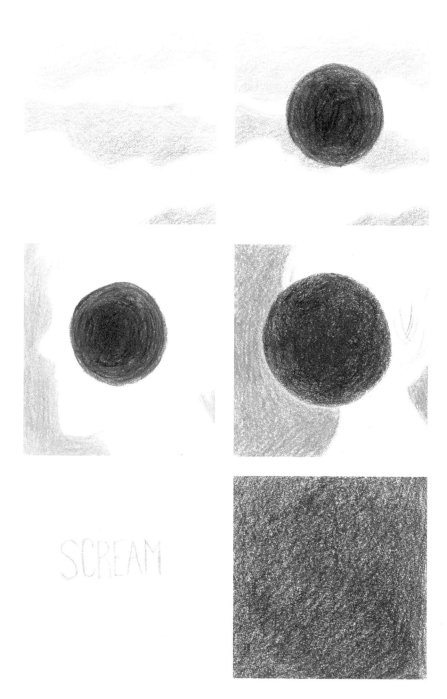

AGAINST THE WIND   AGAINST THE WALL

AGAINST THE SKY

THROW A STONE

INTO THE SKY

HIGH ENOUGH THAT
IT WILL NOT
COME BACK

IMAGINE YOUR
BODY SPREADING
RAPIDLY ALL
OVER THE
WORLD

LIKE THIN TISSUE

YOU'RE STILL SCREAMING

YOUR VOICE IS GETTING HOARSE

(KEEP SCREAMING)

(AS LOUD AS YOU CAN)

THEY WON'T
BE READY

I WISH I COULD
GIVE THEM MORE TIME

AFTER WE HAD BEEN IN THE AIR
FOR A THOUSAND LIFETIMES, WE
STARTED FALLING.

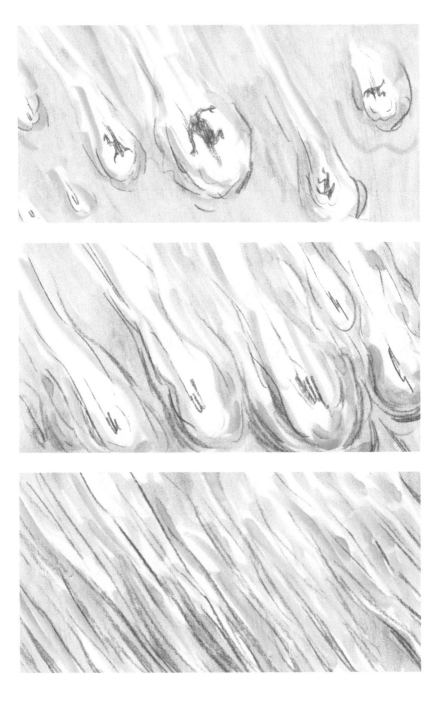

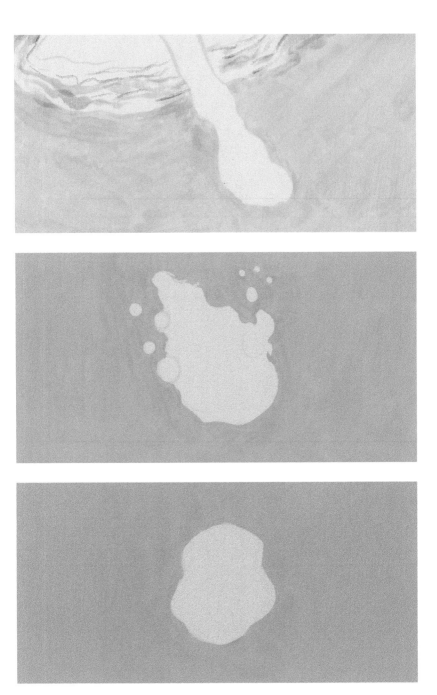

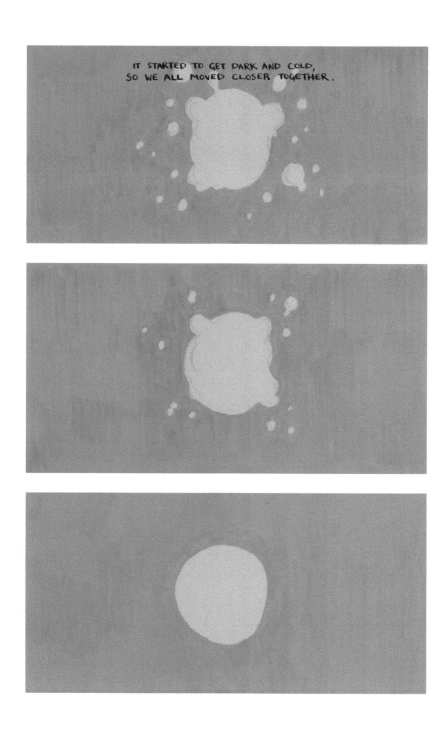

WE REMEMBERED WALKING BAREFOOT ON WET GRASS AND WE REMEMBERED LOSING EVERYTHING.

I GRABBED YOUR HAND AND
I PULLED YOU TOWARDS ME.

IT WAS SO DARK, BUT IF I LOOKED
CLOSELY, I COULD SEE YOU.

I WONDERED IF YOU COULD SEE ME.

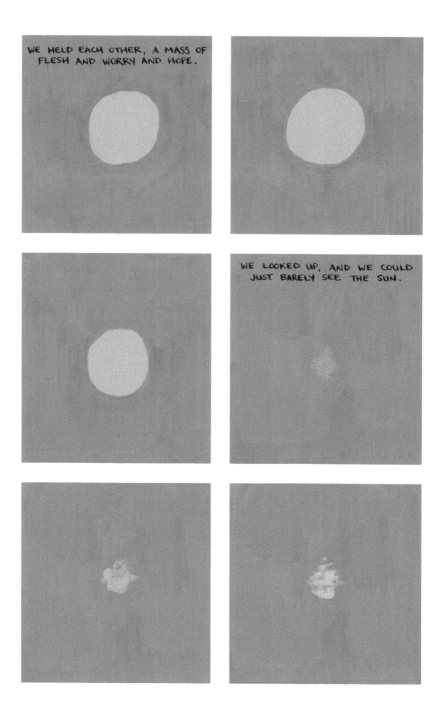

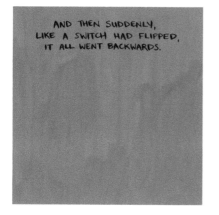

AND THEN SUDDENLY,
LIKE A SWITCH HAD FLIPPED,
IT ALL WENT BACKWARDS.

WE ROSE UP OUT OF THE WATER.

WE WERE PULLED APART
AND THROWN INTO THE SKY.

WE SLAMMED DOWN ONTO THE GROUND
AND WE WERE STUMBLING BACK
INTO OUR OWN FOOTSTEPS.

BUILDINGS BROKE APART
AND HOUSES WERE TORN
DOWN ALL AROUND US.

TREES SHRANK AND
FLOWERS SHRIVELED.

LIFE RUSHED BACK INTO
THROATS AND LUNGS.

WE WERE HURTLING PAST HOPE

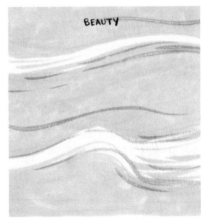

BEAUTY

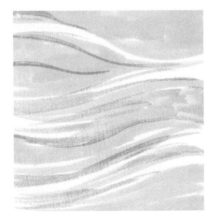

DESPAIR

WE WERE SINGING

SCREAMING

ALL TOGETHER

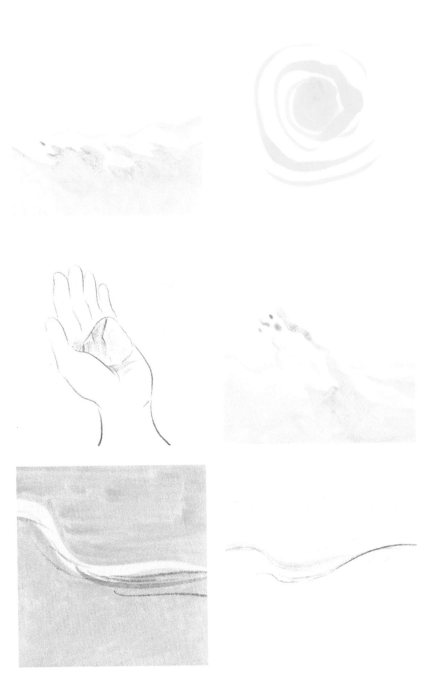

AND THEN

AT THE END, OR AT
THE BEGINNING

IT WAS QUIET

THE ASH TASTED LIKE YESTERDAY
AND THE THINGS WE'D DO DIFFERENT

BUT

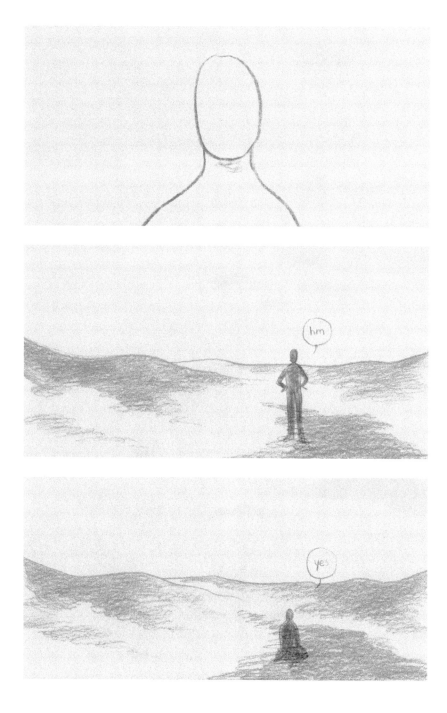

IMAGINE AN ICEBERG,
SHATTERED INTO A
MILLION PIECES

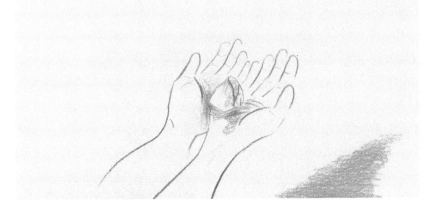

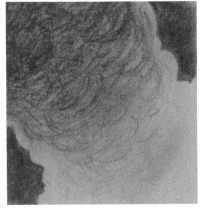

IMAGINE ORANGE SKIES,
THICK WITH FEAR

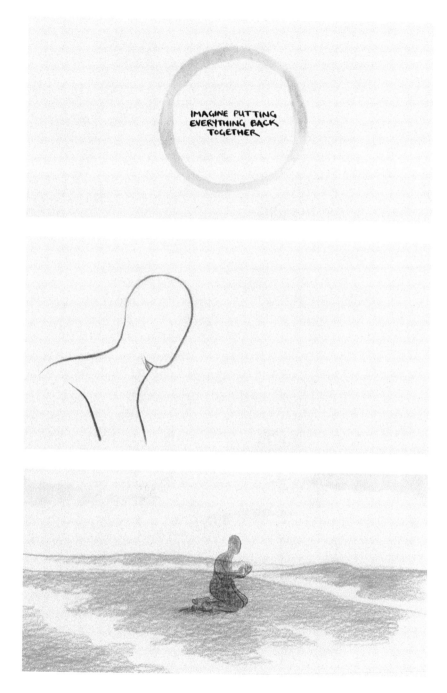

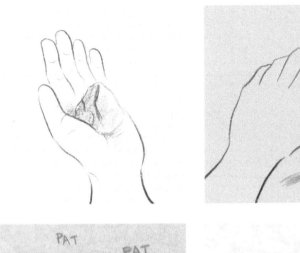

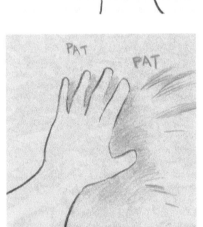

PAT PAT

WE PICKED UP A PENCIL

AND

2015-
2020